BALLAST

B A L L A S T

POEMS

KAREN HOULE

Published in 2000 by
House of Anansi Press Limited
34 Lesmill Road
Toronto, ON M3B 2T6
Tel. (416) 445-3333
Fax (416) 445-5967
www.anansi.ca

Distributed in Canada by
General Distribution Services Ltd.
325 Humber College Blvd.
Etobicoke, ON M9W 7C3
Tel. (416) 213-1919
Fax (416) 213-1917
E-mail cservice@genpub.com

04 03 02 01 00   1 2 3 4 5

CANADIAN CATALOGUING IN PUBLICATION DATA

Houle, Karen
Ballast

ISBN 0-88784-648-3

I. Title.

PS8565.O7735B34 2000   C811'.6   C00-930065-1
PR9199.3.H597B34 2000

Cover design: Angel Guerra
Typesetting: Brian Panhuyzen
Printed and bound in Canada

THE CANADA COUNCIL | LE CONSEIL DES ARTS
FOR THE ARTS | DU CANADA
SINCE 1957 | DEPUIS 1957

We acknowledge for their financial support of our publishing program the Canada
Council for the Arts, the Ontario Arts Council, and the Government of Canada
through the Book Publishing Industry Development Program (BPIDP).

This book is dedicated to
Cézanne Houle and Kuusta Laird
and, a year too late,
Lorna Jean (Black) Dufty.

Contents

bal·last (bal'əst), *n.* [LG.; D. *barlast; bar*, bare, waste + *last*, a load], **1.** anything heavy carried in a ship or vehicle to give stability or in an aircraft to help control altitude. **2.** anything giving stability or firmness to character, human relations, etc. **3.** crushed rock or gravel, as that placed between and below the ties of a railroad. *v.t.* **1.** to furnish with ballast; stabilize. **2.** to fill in (a railroad bed, etc.) with ballast.

— *Webster's New World Dictionary*

Travelling Against

Give me the common or the rare, as they roll.

We are mistaken in what we survive,
in what we must eliminate.

The ladies at the plate glass persist,
reviving their brutal martyrdoms,
worn thin by the abuse of soap,
the contour of teacups in unison

against smallpox, cosmetic agriculture,
and wartime rape. And a woman

they believe unrecognizable
as such.

She is given to volatility around faith.
Faith in where the unlivable gathers

like thistle,
like wild yeast's affinity for chance

Ladies, you know all this. The capture
of your own atrocious beauty
depends upon an unmarked space, a dash
between the certainties you insist
on lighting from the old angle. Your cells

divide, at the physical rate
which you become, or

your old self again: fine pedigrees of cheekbone
and scientific reason. Ahead of wish,
I have survived the common

like a field takes on edges. In humidity,
walk down the middle of alfalfa. The eye
is lamed, when pure absorption
of an acreage heat: I have survived

hydraulic occasions where the purple line
goes white,

where sexual impatience bursts from the sudden rise
like malady. And it is knee-deep

in mustard, in scattered hybrids
of deliberate imperfection.

Slice through against chronicle. Slip your thumb
under the seam where the signal tugs
forward. Pain,

where you grasp it,
is not what you don't want
any more

than an uncontaminated vat remains sterile,
and cannot

Be treated better,
Or promoted across palate.

Be perverse in your indifference to recommend
a local history. Keep the virus for study,
keep this loss of mime. I know

so little,

my arts are often mistaken
in their assemblies, their lambic filiations
among grain and tool. But

it is such hands
as mutate all along the breed,

And travelling against,
And loud.

Ferromagnets, the Everyday Ones, Reverse

I am committed to being in time with you.

We must imagine better than
this hill, this tempo of affection.

Chew the whole of language, incisors
like tongues we will never master all
the shapes of air. Say

a craft, how well we rearranged
the afternoon; its habits, a steady hand
once marshalled our separate skins; and
cupboards, tumbling

onto that moving place
where the mind will not stand still —

stammers, impatient

as Archimedes's complaint. My spine pivots
against the door of your spinning room

and the sun then dropping, dropping,
and the endless varieties of rain.

♦

Nothing retains a former self. Not the smallest
trace, the relic stones are polishing
the bank with constant

misjudgement. Precarious, the waylaid
glacial till, grit such as is taken

the bivalve stomach can conjure
rare earths from the inside,
from here,

this late, late
summer hill

its pearl hollow where the sun can't draw down shade

between this clasp, these clean and perfect days
the lips curl back against.

We find strewn relatives of the former —

dropped out, branched out,
sped up toward
weightlessness

in new places will we be

more than a station, more than happy
to be pinned flat and detailed, as in:

By weight the Earth is mostly iron. The core
having descended more or less in a single glance
through the mantle

to where fire received, with hospitable degree
and some known density, etc.,

we could look up

or just lie back.

There. It wasn't the sky reeling then
it was me or it was you;

and magnetic fields, the everyday ones, reverse.

I read yesterday, the core

of this summer hill
which is flowing

iron, is moving with an independent rotation
overtaking the surface of things

a full lap
once every hundred years or so

it depends on the needle of which instrument,

whether or not
one stays.

How solid that fright
you held up to the window
to verify

we tend toward impending motion, a singed advance
to block the fact of sun,

mostly helium,
devouring itself

It is a matter of the maintenance of speed

over time, this love
is an everyday brand
of parallax, the dual tuning
of gut to drive.

There are no anchored motes
in lucky sequence,

and retold, as in:

Christ delayed his entry into Jerusalem
aboard a certain species of ass. Which had a certain
panoramic fixity; the clinging scent
of worship, tall-tale safe
and sound, as oak

will we be
exposed then
gauge
like trust,

that sense you'll move against my senses —

Such as:

the falling star you said you saw just there.

Stomata

Mark my face with desires like a tribe.

wear down my carpet until
no one can walk without feeling
worn boards on their feet
like time.

Splinter my stairs with your quick beard.

take the laying into the sharpness
of wood as necessity, rounding
the corners we grow
used to

light above the clouds, the slowness
of cells, a buildup
of wax around
stomata:

Breathing there, the book said, exhalation.

Filia

Such mutiny, sister, rarely has the arch
of fury. Blood is physiology
not war, not shovel. Leave this phrase
between us, its difficult grammar.

It is the whole of this that makes us one,

if there's a one, it is what makes us

more than winks of recognition —
one or two bleached baby teeth
in perfume jars,

the amphibious slope
of femaleness, our urgent wrists —

more than the miscellaneous savants
we crowned for their generous remedies

our blood relations circulate

the diagram
of what burns between us,

intact and sweet-smelling
as home,

the metaphor a heart takes turns with.

The intimate oscillations of unlikeness. The gap is
fatal, a gun-grey crust
our cut-out faces
press against.

How you drape all this with grand texture —

cause and effect
transform by unravelling
birth and death
some sororal archive.

I have rarely felt such permanent failure

of touchstone as this, the flight of rain;

the damaged feldspar gleams
the best possible red
this creek will ever conjure

◆

sympathetic magic, dulled plain
by the pocket's amnesia,

or, the diction of air; air more crucial
than this temporary kindness.

◆

Sometimes I must be allowed to leave you.

Sometimes, forgetting plot is best,

the work of killing, by mistake,
is gentle —

The blistering comes late, blistering in hard
and tuneless holidays
we hammer out

a welcome for the tribe
who'll jam the station, who'll scale the beachhead
sorted by colour or by age.

A clan.

This is the art of incursive genealogy:
a million years to move one hundred

random bones set by decorum
at arbitrary angles to the whole. Such as:

he, olive-skinned and twenty
        of apparent Egyptian
        descent, his shadow's slant
        illegible,

undisciplined as children's gardening.

◆

Must we interrogate the rotation of the Earth

that we might live in this world
and both be beautiful? Your husband's feathered
hand sometimes strays

toward my complicated back—

◆

Filia:

what could we pretend to,
from time to time

I want to live in the elation
of open water, high and climbing
like the lapping heat of wine.

I want to live where I will name my family
by their carefulness with rice,
and sandstone fossils —

the ones my green eyes treasure in the railbed.

And those who love the world's full belly —

rolling, coral, sudden
as a barn swallow plays the eaves;

and vulnerable, as pitch of roof, to hail.

Müller's Finches

Ice freezes at 273 degrees Kelvin.

Nothing moves,
there is nothing left

for the finches to stay the winter fat
but that I share my bread.

Weren't Darwin's lot a marvel? Toolbox
torqued beaks, any number
of professions —

the soil, the clouds, the whole edible zone
wrenched wide-open.

◆

Between the trade winds and this window

there must have been a freak storm
veering off its designated slope —

For I am cold here
on the warm side of the glass.

The hellish birds out there
already starving. They'll snap

directly at the frozen crust: ice and feed
two perfect whites

discerned only by relative resistance.

◆

Let's not fool ourselves:

Whatever takes a single shape
does but depend.

My hand, the old style, adept
at helpmate

such as is programmed
down to the smallest detail.

My handsome tribe, viz. female
as feedline:

a constant, paring motion
through diverse hunger.

How the palm and mouth rock
back and forth across

the vague ideas of prey, feast
wearing down its fine metal teeth.

Skill has a look.

And conducts herself accordingly:

She sits and, measured, watches.
She flies up all at once.

Ballast

The harvest is not autumnal, it is
in the kitchen, all the guests
like same sheaves.

The face, it takes
a minute to know, is yours. It heaves
me out of a straight line, a story
I was maybe telling.

Like an unsuspecting bulb
your frost. My guesses wild, my
hands loose as spring thaw.

And putting all this into a tube.
The evening bends
within the noise

of our tenants loving upstairs. If only
I knew her nose, I would see it flare
under his shape.

It fires me
beyond the grain of sleep: what I know
of him, what I imagine
in the dirt thin sheets.

What is the space left by leaving?

There is something to the bend
of your brow, a gate between your brow
and his inclination to know
how uncontained I am.

Knit me a task here,

Make it patterned. I'll follow easily
those trails like rhododendrons
budding ferocious, and courage
across the winter's long-held breath.

Wolves weren't so fluid
as the moment you touched the back of your neck;

its shuddering brownness —

there is no place
on Earth, no place
on my continent

between two tough tides —

How can I be certain of not nothingness?

The Mormon Cricket

In a complicated set of moods
the Mormon cricket insists

on passage. Distended abdomen
of the nearest male

thickens; that is,
fixes surplus —

Where there will be feeding from.

Astride him, impolite,
she eats him;

which is to say, sweet enough.

◆

in field guides
in herbal lore

Clean-cut vistas sort the ranks:

lowly grasses trail glory-
throated orchids. And in the upstanding
plant community such indiscretions
as a trolling wasp

are known to try
a field's conviction.

♦

once for grain
once for miracle

Thick, rude strokes burrow into backlit skin.

The longhand arithmetic of leavening

posts a cheap asymmetry
to the rapid fire of
circumstance —

Three million authorized cricket cells
turn on a dime.

Mechanism or sacrament or despair: Either way,

the active gamble
tends to sink in, closing
its wake behind.

Magicicada septendecim

The giant cicada emerges once every seventeen years.

Up corkless trunks the charmless larvae
drain all fluids. They intercept. They tap
a Morse code for every possible prey:

They travel confident.

The way they have timed their falling-out with the world —

both grand and intimate. They invent predicament
and then outlive it. Strategies of flesh

cannot be rehearsed, the game
is wedded to ceremony for the hero and the foe,
for what words of comfort suit their vocation
for order. I will not let you play adversary:

You promised me a plain, original pleasure.

I will exact it from you, because we are able

Because flesh wounds need not be sutured
to the old couplets by the kind of knots we know.

◆

Neither this fallen plum nor this rancid sap
are as useless as the occult we share.

I don't recall the occidental word for culprit,

my daughters might. That I have two is rarely
the point. Small women thread needles

by licking, which seems, from this far up the dynasty,
a hundred miles, accurate, and industrious: A loop

is made by the tip, on the soft inside.

◆

What we cannot know to see we should surrender
to touch: the metal eye and its edge of error
are poised and empty —

They can avoid it without looking; use
the thumb's membrane, drumming
stillness. And in the giving dark

we could know the clattering of certainty.

◆

So I stung hard.

And saw one man lose his life to stubborn chemistry.

The maypole bees have a histamine queen
who knows the cardinal points of the sun,

and they die for her too, throughout the reign of workdays.

In these ways the sky suffers
the operative geometries of trait, imposed, some say,
in order for us to dance,

and food

seems to understand
its way in, then branch stylishly
into water or waste. The brass edibles
weighed for incidental dangers:

pollen, ergot, mercury

stored like fat to test the heat
swims back around your blood
in August

the month you finally lash your bones
with gristle,

with unreasonable joy
straying toward displays of death.

Lay me again
in the regular wedges of leftover warmth —

It's early on, the drones will feed themselves below.

Such a love might fester, might percolate down
the tiered inventions of the vast cicada world.

♦

It is not a failing
to leave the word for luck out of recipe

Look there:

Bystander ants receive an honest amber day.

Lord hear me out:

My loves are undisciplined, they roll
between the will of thread and the litany
of routine suggestions for the good life.

My almanac, I confess, is quite punctual:

Tomorrow I have given up, I claim, for good. If
this is heaven, then this is undecided —

as far as it goes
it is a very careful love.

Catalogue

there is still space in the fields.
there is air, plenty,

you need not crouch, you need not sit
so still and unpleasant
inside a crack of quiet, you learned lately.

that tractor's slivering blades forget
the intimate touch of history. crass
shards of pots beyond catalogue, ossified
crows cut even by suggestion of blade.

a bone of christ carried here.
in stomach, in saliva,

you are silver or tooth or cobalt. the accidental
lies so silent, crouched like a molar
into the swing of the undisturbed hinge:

femur, I finger its diamond once
marrow. rooms out or in are thickened
by motes, the same clock, your hands
in the morning prior to your desk.

and once you begin to take things out.

out of ridges, furrows of keep. gravity
pulling things into the lonely space I once had
a right to say something about my own past.

do not align even once what you are placing
about here. do not align.

The Sign for Double Endlessness

To practise your arrival I just kept moving

the impending day back
a week or so, a letter.

Moving my wrists in Gaussian swipes
I gutted your waiting bedroom

its cloistered layers, the papery weft
of all the ones who slept
before you. It takes

three hours to refuse
floral pasts tell a moving story; just one
short time, in figure eights,

I gashed my thumb deep
and strange: the blade strained
toward its love of angled,
more precise work.

Paper, like ice, mutters as it swells and
curls away

And us
And the ancient glue

does not receive impetuous white,
the ugly streaks, like April light, or

morning already, the
morning already you're here.

◆

Here, and not immunity. The rough outline
shovelled under late fall shoulder blades,
solvent

with the anxious gain: Hold us,

as houses are given to
as paper is given to

be lived out: speech, sleep, signature.

◆

Later, we'll rub out clean; less encyclopedic claims
will be made.

Rock, as category,

is largely based upon the power to hold two tight
particulate histories —

those poised and granular attempts
deposited the length

one goes to master

the lived-in pace of inventory. Daily

I practised your leaving,
like piano, to perfection.

for love
for style

you take a strong arm to it.

Undertow

In effect we find the sketches of invention:

a waterproof book, cross-wired for gold thread balance,
the key to doing many things at once.

But in the standard silver photo
her back is turned to me:

upright as premonition in emulsion's freckling grain.

Your hand is going for her hair,
your face exactly halfway

between a flood of light and a momentary dark, a cloud
which was not a cloud but me

starting out from where anyone starts out.

You met her later in Switzerland, and I have practised
the name like undertow, and mostly in the legs,

a name which never matches the imagined,
the legendary pull of water.

Surface Tension: Three Crossings

Surface tension

is a vaguely dotted line
you set aside

its details, face down
like sea ice, the weight

distributed evenly
across the wagon-full, titanium
amphorae, charged with
particles of radon-coloured
dirt, which,

in the work of discovery
cannot resist
putting to the tongue:

arsenic; apparently
the Pythians had begun
to mark their dead.

A custodial respect

for open water
takes us
out over it.

She was tempted, but not fatal.
That same open water

figured daily in her,
measured

crossing meant twenty-one
hours in a red bathing suit,

in eels
ribboned at the hip
without saying how

she would eventually
be pulled from the lake.

Shapes are collecting
hundreds deep, where metal
conserves without apparent loss
the sunlight bends

when pieces stop falling.

Small damp coins, loosed
from inverted pockets —

two maybe three dives per diem.

Phoenician walleyed
sponge divers recognize
copper ingots minutes past
lung capacity

is a spinning downward,
is an inaudible
coming to rest, to thicken
the buildup

like hope or research will,
on clean flat surfaces —

All these will have to be weighed.

Having confessed
to having no recollection —

the flick that moves the silt
from front to back, pretends
to be a cup, quick —

she gives a little wave
for the camera. "Oh,

that's how it ends," she says.
"I had no idea."

Looking right at you, she breaks
the alert ropes, extending

a special kind of complication

breaks the days and nights
among the long practice,
the uninterrupted plunge

in sleep, in oxygen
all the way to the bottom

it's sheer approximation

of when, a generous hint of magnitude
straightens momentarily
a stray hair, cutlery;

having taken on too much

some say warship
some say trade

leaned wide over the basin, then
listed to the right, like a laugh
ducks down awkward
under the clavicle:

the V-shaped bones distinguishing
in us an up from down.

Hands will do, and do
stumble in air, and salt;

in exhaustion

I have come far enough to believe
she was blank.

Circling blank is simple motion

well beyond the five or six, the
still-to-go: it's when you've
set aside the count.

Logic

Full-blown love has no history,
only a birth and a logic.

No rare preconditions, no random
leathered shame straying
at the places of deepest manufacture.

Let a single shade dominate
the prehistory we might tell:

The deepest arch
from the cellarway was always
a bending in, a bending back.

Would we dwell then in the gift
of pastlessness? Free or impotent

to domesticate my sex
worn thin on the rim
of your neck.

Violent riddles of intimacy
and fortune: Take revenge
on the homelessness we will be cast
after years of taking this
as mere.

Tiptoe from this open room

swinging to sleep, memory: Take no interest
in chalk marks, in ink or page.

Stride past me straight to history.

Palmistry

The largest organ infiltrates the lifeline,
it comes to be read

like the constant press from various dirt,
unthought contact

with surfaces travelling over, foreign
and incalculable.

I didn't set it up before.
It wasn't in the book.

Planes are leaving hourly from the opposite bank;

provisions, maps, and spares
aped from every previous
disaster.

I never swore that with these palms we would find
what had been declared fit for search.

1620 (Moosonee, Ontario)

in the dead of winter moosonee looks like it did in 1620. no
lights across the way, no rock. just sand washing into the delta.

i hire a wrinkly red man's freighter canoe. we head for moose
factory, slicing the snow-grooved river.

against the blackness i make out tribal remains. logs sink
into sinking ground and it is a hospital for dying red people
full of needing Hospital.

the east hills ache to form cliffs. the scaffolding around the ridge
stops the ski-doos. when you dive two things will help you:
the greenness of the water, and the black spruce growing up
fast under the surface. make an arc with your body when you
go down, thrown by ski-doo or just wanting to. turn fast, chase
the bubbles up. avoid the sap: it tricks you into staying down.
there are no fish anymore, just places to play.

the hotel owner brings young red-brown girls into her office.
"Tropic of Cancer" is tattooed over her nippleless left breast.
the girls say she never been tugged at by milky mouth. her
right breast has a wrapping of chocolate-coloured skin, and
when she moves their hands along that which is like their own,
which is like their own.

the white fingernail of a beach clipped between the foot
of the cliff and the dock. how will i hide the sickly yellowness
of my hair? i cut branches and make a cage, a green cage. i glide
toward the ceremony fastened to the bank like low tide.

the oneida are fierce, the mennonites are gentle. the black
figures at the summer village are crows. in the short tuck
of summer children wrestle with upright weathered logs.
regret: i may never understand the rules.

my whole body knows. here, a wall of cedar sticks,
carved up totems. at the tip: a circle of stars and feather. i jump
and come down. and jump again, higher each time
until i hover at the apex shedding gravity and my green cage
like a snakeskin. kwakiutl women gather round.
their sun faces glint, watching me climb.

level with the eyes of the bird of flight. i reach out and tuck it
into the folds of my hair which turns the shade of
the bird, of the women, nutmeg sparrows.

an artifact in the gravel. a fat boy runs up and asks if it is *istassin*,
fake. i say yes. (a lie.) i hold hudson's astrolab in my cold
cold hands and the magic does not leave me though
the cadence of my tongue makes the red man's boat
falter on the water.

Hotel woman and i. Hospital procedures after sickness.
how we scour blood out of chesterfields and hallways. the
louvred doors a trick of open and shut. how we bury our own
dead swearing for this world to pass. how they bury their
dead in moose factory.

Ornithology

Three small blackbirds took the last giant one down.

When it struck the earth the petals moved off their tulips
and waded deep into the straw.

Animals of the ground, animals of modest proportion
tried to mate with the fallen yellow thing

now trussed and folded and swollen with gravity.

They tried to take it into their own bodies
through any hole, and burrow deep
the yellow spark, the flight-drenched seeds —

Anything to lift them from ten generations
in the ring, the brass clean ring.

♦

Then the three blackbirds who operate
shared the breast and the wishbone
and the saffron-tinted sash among themselves,

not from an innate love of colour
but straightaway gizzard and size of appetite.

◆

After, there were stray feathers, cupped
and moving close to the ground, still
warm with contempt
for their brightly shining limits.

These, I came out of hiding for.

These, I hid in the swollen stamens
of the blue-backed tulips:

imports, cross-eyed beauties
locked in their strange fecundity.

◆

The following season I crept from the basin
one last time

to watch the yellow pollen,
the staining yellow going up.

Ephemeroptera (the "Burrowing Mayfly")

Is this how light you can be, and still furious?

With my haptic eye, the squid-black
vitreous one, I saw them flock like panned gold
at the slow bottom thaw,

nickering when the birch pollen
seeped down towel-thick
enough for the climes to roll:

widemouthed particles of spring.

They took up all at once for the shallows,

a hastily acquired love of light,
clattering spoons on the morning surface.

Though I didn't blink or shut my skin,
what cued their strict desire

to that grey depth, with that precision?

75,000,000 (Brooks, Alberta)

Therefore only river and air carry the whole machine:

colour, speed, shape
bound together like October
nails a hammer to its own repeating blows

off the red-brick roof, and downstream
centuries-old seepage buckles
softness by penetration

of the water table. A clear
record can then be made if and only if
a needle shadows true to ridge;

if it shoves the digit back.

◆

The king is bound to the long bones of himself, muted
claws, his skull and spine gagged
in the wolf willows
like swimmers' clothes;

a compound beast hence liquid chromatography:

flight, protein, dive.

The frothing geological trance thickens
to paste; inside the slowing down
whose fingerprints besides,

trapped under a freshly licked edge?

◆

What settles out intact is shape —

that special branch
designed to whip the retina
like tag alder —

the hardest parts held up

like wedding rings
to house fires

(a fine narrow band).

Tractor, Ledger

The machine that dares you to lie down in a field:

It is ledger-ready; it is spring.

It is rusty fringed with lockjaw edges,
the shiny winged fenders
girls go jiggly on, riding
dangerously young.

March, dribbling down the front, knuckles humping
around the endless work like loaves.

A wafer-thin disc lifting and lifting
the trachea's diesel skirts up
the scowling day

and blank, unfeeling sky. Flushed-out starling
varieties whorl like fingerprints, they are chasing
something new

or something old. Thumbnails
split vertically: beech and seven-cord
cruelty that pools in the head

such as is discipline.

When summer comes we drive the bent blue truck
on pock-faced roads

just looking for a turnaround or
an ancient site to rummage.

Once upon just such a trip I found a broken teapot
with black pansy eyes, it lies
in my bottom drawer.

(And spent shells.)

◆

The classic warning is metallic, rising
off the back of the throat.

The grammatical rule: Give way —

(You were a surveyor, too, in the nurse-room
poplars where dime leaves turned
to shake off dust.)

Ever since

those nervous machines, those gentlemen
who hauled the road this far, in fluid
sections drained the woods

after a brief but practised
estimate of length.

To have learned that this applies
to deer, to ditch —

whatever slows the hewer's front.

Clydesdales

That frozen pond day, a full calendar from knowing
he was deaf,

Tobias slipped under the paddock fence and ran
among the Clydesdales, the ones with breath in winter
like a whole, bronze world.

The headstrong wind emptied our mouths, the headstrong
girl, fingers strung to his, she knew
he was not afraid.

    His eyes were dead calm, unlaced.
    He seemed to be coming out from there.
    Or something equally still, asking:

What else comes from where this breath comes from?

Sumac

You are never sure.

The names of fish that dart, or if
the cedar fists hide a stone bridge
from you. A stone-cold

slab of creek, your new knife's tip plunges between
the ribs of July heat.

This current is stronger than your stroke.

Here, you are not sure.

The hidden drive pins behind
the cedar's private arms, you hadn't imagined this
gaping,

headlights massacre the splintered barn, they're
on their way —

Suddenly you know.

The light is failing.

You, this solvent universe, this backseat
leans against a pressing green,
the pressing green like corn.

◆

What matters, then, is training:

the hand to take to wheel, unmediated, soundless
click of habit sailing right on through,
steadied in the properties of oil.

What matters is what goes where:

is where and why the day goes,
is how the living sugars picked up speed

in the flat stretch way back of the dark wire
forfeit runs like oxide, patterning
the unmarked curve, the *coming-up-too-fast*
memory spilling regular as bales.

♦

You might have heard the river's sighs
pulled one by one, splintered panic
reeds against your sunburned forehead —

their wide-eyed sped-up *right-behind-you* scent.

♦

Here, a simple day unspools

your copper longing
uncreased morning's lap
iron-red with hot beginning
pulled you

midday, starts out, simply

met you

going the other way.

Didn't you let it take you?

Riddle you with dust, you barely recollect,
the slimmest light, a sharp horizontal, the glove box

that goes out.

You couldn't see

how each attempt is both an opening and a closing.

No end to it.

◆

The shape of nothing in an unpresuming palm
strikes all at once: not the tentative,
murk-bound embrace
like fish and hook,

the strike is sudden, like the baby's kick will be

And unprovoked. It spurs in you a raw distrust
of dance, northern-styled arithmetic
held to the power of ten.

You know that long eyes burn with such looking?

♦

Tonight you'll learn the roads by scent:

Since shifting fuel evaporates all trace
of signs, then what you thought you knew
will stand in good enough for map.

Careful.

Your last month's turpentine wants its duty crass
down there among the ditched and the relentless
local weeds.

Remember that dog-eared day you spied the merciless
red of sumac?

You were coming up the creek-gouged bank,
wet hair and planning straight for home —

(how there was something red and turning over
their engines.)

How somehow you knew to run?

Long Division
(for Lisa)

Before even he had gauged its shivering precise path,

I saw her limbs receiving the superficial mark,
the impertinent nick of entry.

This earned for me a portion of his awkward trust.

Am I the engineer of trembling luck, of uncareful voltages,
his optimism worn thin as family myelin?

His shoulders are drawn against a common form of shame;

they'll snap in two along the perforations
he has planned out belonging.

Would that this night's rest and then the next hold its
old velocity;

that she sleep soundly, oblivious to the forking series
of dashes his claims emit

a pivotal newness
a long and absolute rest —

an otherwise ordinary afternoon.

Threshold

All along I thought I heard them practise love.

Soft as dry rot, down the stairwell,
giving in, like basement to water,
to wood, a thousand or so
termites gnawing a shape
for matrimony.

A rhythmic thud, each morning, the empty feet
swing down, the cold wooden floor;
the lowest grade of light,
is bare,

is no more suited to what I thought was love,

than to what I thought were stars,

the temperament
of the main-sequence
nebulae,

or:

phenomena clearly visible to the naked eye; ringed,
flat on their back, and consoled
by an inattentive flare,

a lone heart, white ash,
travelling down the bald sky
banister at higher speeds
than I can divide.

◆

How many loosened thresholds, pried and coming
toward, the lights left on,
polite

for night travel. A million gypsy moths
to eat the temporary remainders
of a readied dark.

Winged and shelled and weightless. Nothing more,

Nothing less fatal than those portions
of weary light laid out along-
side your lover's shoes —

their dust-creased insistence on
an outside world, another possible world.

♦

The small and solid shape a promise makes
descending in the mouth;
the roundness

o:

it's steady work

keeping lead-lined nights
fastened down to wish.

♦

A minor wind emits a gamma shower
swaybacked laugh, hey

there's the evening star.

Jay, Breaking

There's an echo a jay makes, breaking from a branch.

There was a shop open late, I drank
straight from the freezer, an unhesitating,
indivisible motion—

(walking, are you prone to dilute
emptiness with speed?)

I would have liked to stop all at once
to ask the grocer about the olives
and which day he had seen you last

like I did—full-length, pulled-down pistil days,
oxblood velvet to the very top, rows and rows

(and what had kept them there?). The brine, the glacial
till maligned rusted air, an upward tempo

like the Adriatic lifts
a heavy lid.

There is a rhythm sandals slap an open-toed return,
vaguely like return; cooled-down sidewalks,

the barebacked story hour—

whatever we make up to make it real.

The Scarlet Mallow

opens white, at dawn, but turns within the hour
since heat can drag a promise

from a name. Far from equatorial, it is simply
breakfast, the saltshaker, you hold
out your hand —

things, each time, an emptiness can open

the door. Careful as a pair of robin's eggs: one blue
and one blue, it gets crowded
in a kitchen,

in rooms, and how they touch you, yet keep their parts.

♦

Then an early, sudden storm. The buzz of nitrogen
anointment: things hunker down
like toads' poor strategies with noise;

prostrate, as Low German, feeling for the contours
of the thing itself.

◆

But prone to retreat. Were it not the case, I saw it moving
with my own hands —

those tell-tale scarlet seams, warming
to a pale cup.

Lift

The first day that street was with us
I knew east and west as the opening
of ankles, falling toward rest.

Waking, I saw they were taking the statues
across the littered churchyard; by cranes,
by crates, they were lashing
a length of gate to plank.

The mute past at every step
that is the same,

and then
is not,

is looping like expensive trains, plush
and aproned to the Seine like ribs.

Pious magnolias, we spied, each park,
their stainless gloves clenched —

It was Easter

coming loose a day or two before
what we tend to register as spring.

Those greasy buds unwound for days
among themselves, the dark cores
that held them at their belts, notched
since they were born.

The shrewd crowbars fluttered down
the early light above the churchyard's
silence; you slept right past
the alarm

that thick canopy muffles, false promises
shuffling along: for health, a city
cuts back hard.

Bread, handsaws, secateurs clipped the iron bells
swung thickly, and swung true; the abbé's sash—

Imagine the plans he might have had
for such a falling-out?

Jackknife

You have never watched me do the backstroke.

I won marathons in unnamed lakes up and down
my landlocked childhood,

and you (who are taken by
the troubling work of insects, where immunization
is the norm), it seems you're going.

I taught myself a special sidestroke for scissoring away
from all that inattention. The fitting glove
was in the shadow of the diving board.

All night long I dove to the bottom of the pool
for your belongings: You complied,
because there's a certain safety in dryness.

This I have learned to expect.

When I don't look I can't tell where my watch is.
Plus, the peril of loudspeaker announcements
usually pertains to either you or me. Is there still time

to comb the bottom for the missing halves of earrings?

Semiprecious, but I know the general whereabouts;
conditions of the local bays, a jackknife
prod like late prospects near the early hours,

when I abandoned all hope of the return
of swim trunks. It's easier to find you

with my skin.

Acknowledgements

Warm thanks for their efforts and support: Janice Kulyk Keefer, Patrick Lane, Tim Lilburn, Di Brandt, the Sage Hill Writing Experience, Ellen Seligman, Mani Haghighi, Arlene Lampert, John Hurd, and Jay Lampert. I would also like to acknowledge the financial contributions of the departments of English and Philosophy, University of Guelph.